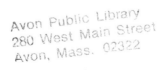

Goin' to Boston

An Exuberant Journey in Song

For our friends in Boston
—H. E. M.
—E. B.

Text copyright © 2002 by H. Ellen Margolin
Illustrations copyright © 2002 by Emily Bolam
CIP Data is available
All rights reserved
Published in the United States 2002 by Handprint Books
413 Sixth Avenue, Brooklyn, New York 11215
www.handprintbooks.com

First Edition
Printed in China
ISBN: 1-929766-45-9
10 9 8 7 6 5 4 3 2 1

Goin' to Boston

An Exuberant Journey in Song

H. Ellen Margolin

illustrated by

Emily Bolam

HANDPRINT BOOKS   BROOKLYN, NEW YORK

Good-bye, Pappy,
I'm goin' to Boston,

Good-bye, Pappy,
I'm goin' to Boston,
Good-bye, Pappy,
I'm goin' to Boston,
Ear-lye in the morning.

Saddle up, boys, and let's go with her,
Saddle up, boys, and let's go with her,
Saddle up, boys, and let's go with her,
Ear-lye in the morning.

Won't we look pretty on the Common,
Won't we look pretty on the Common,
Won't we look pretty on the Common,
Ear-lye in the morning.

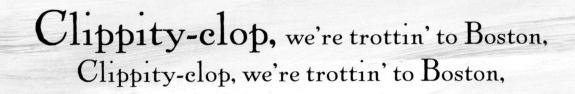

Clippity-clop, we're trottin' to Boston,
Clippity-clop, we're trottin' to Boston,

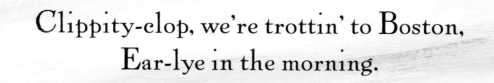

Clippity-clop, we're trottin' to Boston,
Ear-lye in the morning.

Wave good-bye, we're goin' to Boston,
Wave good-bye, we're goin' to Boston,
Wave good-bye, we're goin' to Boston,
Ear-lye in the morning.

Won't we look pretty on the Common,
Won't we look pretty on the Common,
Won't we look pretty on the Common,
Ear-lye in the morning.

Bouncy, bouncy, we'll get to Boston,
Bouncy, bouncy, we'll get to Boston,

Bouncy, bouncy, we'll get to Boston,
Ear-lye in the morning.

They're still
behind us.

Follow, follow, we're half-way to Boston,
Follow, follow, we're half-way to Boston,

Follow, follow, we're half-way to Boston,
Ear-lye in the morning.

Beepity-beep, we're goin' to Boston,
Beepity-beep, we're goin' to Boston,
Beepity-beep, we're goin' to Boston,
Ear-lye in the morning.

Wait
for
me!

Won't we look pretty on the Common,
Won't we look pretty on the Common,
Won't we look pretty on the Common,
Ear-lye in the morning.

Round and round, we're dancin' to Boston,
Round and round, we're dancin' to Boston,

Round and round, we're dancin' to Boston,
Ear-lye in the morning.

Swingin', swingin', all the way to Boston,
Swingin', swingin', all the way to Boston,

Swingin', swingin', all the way to Boston,
Ear-lye in the morning.

Won't we look pretty on the Common,
Won't we look pretty on the Common,
Won't we look pretty on the Common,
Ear-lye in the morning.

Giddy-up, horsie, we're comin' to Boston,
Giddy-up, horsie, we're comin' to Boston,

HOORAY!

Giddy-up, horsie, we're comin' to Boston,
Ear-lye in the morning.

We're on Boston Common!

Fresh Apples

Round and round, we'll keep on dancin',
Round and round, we'll keep on dancin',
Round and round, we'll keep on dancin',
Ear-lye in the morning.

Don't we look pretty on the Common,
Don't we look pretty on the Common,
Don't we look pretty on the Common,

Ear-lye in the morning!

Goin' to Boston

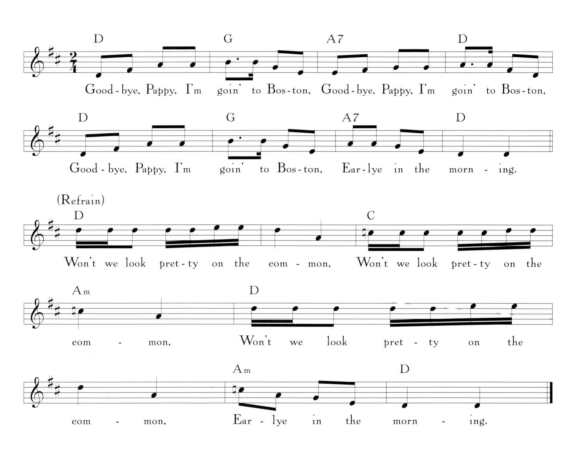

Good - bye, Pappy, I'm goin' to Bos - ton, Good - bye, Pappy, I'm goin' to Bos - ton,

Good - bye, Pappy, I'm goin' to Bos - ton, Ear - lye in the morn - ing.

(Refrain)

Won't we look pret - ty on the com - mon, Won't we look pret - ty on the

com - mon, Won't we look pret - ty on the

com - mon, Ear - lye in the morn - ing.

Saddle up, boys, and let's go with her,
Saddle up, boys, and let's go with her,
Saddle up, boys, and let's go with her,
Ear-lye in the morning.
 **REFRAIN**

Clippity-clop, we're trottin' to Boston,
Clippity-clop, we're trottin' to Boston,
Clippity-clop, we're trottin' to Boston,
Ear-lye in the morning.
 **REFRAIN**

Wave good-bye, we're goin' to Boston,
Wave good-bye, we're goin' to Boston,
Wave good-bye, we're goin' to Boston,
Ear-lye in the morning.
REFRAIN

Bouncy, bouncy, we'll get to Boston,
Bouncy, bouncy, we'll get to Boston,
Bouncy, bouncy, we'll get to Boston,
Ear-lye in the morning.
REFRAIN

Follow, follow, we're half-way to Boston,
Follow, follow, we're half-way to Boston,
Follow, follow, we're half-way to Boston,
Ear-lye in the morning.
REFRAIN

Beepity-beep, we're goin' to Boston,
Beepity-beep, we're goin' to Boston,
Beepity-beep, we're goin' to Boston,
Ear-lye in the morning.
REFRAIN

Round and round, we're dancin' to Boston,
Round and round, we're dancin' to Boston,
Round and round, we're dancin' to Boston,
Ear-lye in the morning.
REFRAIN

Swingin', swingin', all the way to Boston,
Swingin', swingin', all the way to Boston,
Swingin', swingin', all the way to Boston,
Ear-lye in the morning.
REFRAIN

Giddy-up, horsie, we're comin' to Boston,
Giddy-up, horsie, we're comin' to Boston,
Giddy-up, horsie, we're comin' to Boston,
Ear-lye in the morning.
REFRAIN

Round and round, we'll keep on dancin',
Round and round, we'll keep on dancin',
Round and round, we'll keep on dancin',
Ear-lye in the morning.
REFRAIN

Author's Note

"Going to Boston" is an old Appalachian song that is about the Common in either Boston, Massachusetts, or Boston in the East Midlands of England. No one is sure which of the parks is being celebrated.

I first heard it sung by a guitar-playing music teacher who was explaining the intricacies of a square dance to a group of boys and girls. The first verse and the refrain stayed in my memory, and I used those words as a starting point for this book. I added other verses to advance the action and bring all the characters together on Boston Common.

The Boston Common is America's oldest public park. John Winthrop and his Puritan followers first encamped there in 1630. The local Indians called the place Shawmutt, meaning "living waters." The Puritans renamed it Boston, after a town in England.

The Puritans were accustomed to having "common land" set aside for everyone to use. Goats, sheep, and cows grazed; the militia marched, sometimes accompanied by band music. And in a time when there were no jails, where was the best place to punish wrong-doers? The Common!

In Boston, Massachusetts, animals grazed on the Common until 1830, when they were no longer permitted, probably for sanitary reasons.

In the 1600s no one strolled on the Common on Sunday—almost everybody went to Church. Now Sunday is the Common's busiest day as families enjoy the lawns, the walking paths, the statues—perhaps a picnic lunch.

I can watch children splash in the water at the Frog Pond in summer and ice-skate there in winter. I have played Frisbee on the lawn and have stopped to hear a soapbox orator or a street musician. And on many a summer evening, I've parked my car in the underground lot beneath the Common and went above to hear a free outdoor concert.

Over time, a common evolves and is used for many different purposes. The grown-ups and children depicted in this book represent more than two hundred years of varied activities.

Thanks to the English and to our first settlers, many towns and cities have central open spaces, which remain quiet and green, even when urban development crowds around them.

—H. E. M.